T S

DAISY KUTTER

THE LAST TRAIN

WRITTEN & ILLUSTRATED BY
KAZU KIBUISHI

Published by Viper Comics

Jessie Garza, president & publisher

Jim Resnowski, creative director & editor-in-chief

Viper Comics
9400 N. MacArthur Blvd. Ste. #124-215
Irving, TX 75063
USA

www.vipercomics.com

Second Edition: August 2006
ISBN 0-9754193-2-3

Printed in the USA

CONTENTS

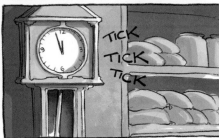

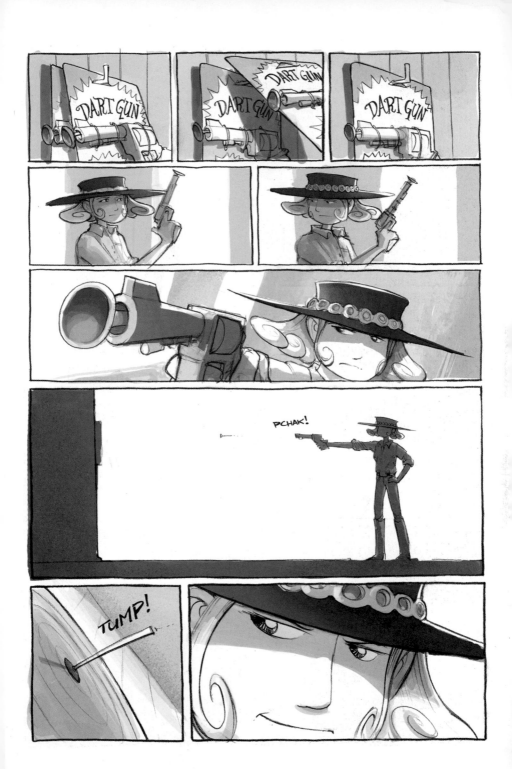

HEY DAISY.

WHAT THE HELL DO YOU WANT, TOM?

EVERY TIME I SHOW UP AROUND HERE, YOU MAKE IT SOUND LIKE SOMETHING JUST **DIED.**

SERIOUSLY, WHAT DO YOU **WANT?**

A COUPLE OF GUYS HAVE BEEN MILLING ABOUT TOWN AND I RECOGNIZED THEM FROM THE MOST WANTED LIST. I OVERHEARD THEM MENTION YOUR NAME A FEW TIMES.

JUST WONDERING IF, Y'KNOW, YOU WERE BACK IN THE **GAME.**

IF BY "GAME", YOU MEAN DRY GOODS SALES, THEN **YEAH.**

PCHINK!

YOU KNOW WHAT I MEAN.

I TOLD YOU I QUIT, DIDN'T I?

I JUST HAD A FEELING YOU MIGHT BE GETTING A LITTLE ANTSY.

I CAN HANDLE IT.

I WAS ALSO WONDERING IF YOU WOULD BE INTERESTED IN JOINING ME AT SHELLY'S FOR POKER NIGHT.

AS SHERIFF, SHOULDN'T YOU BE STAYING AWAY FROM THE TABLES?

OH. I WON'T BE PLAYING, OF COURSE. I'LL BE MARSHALLING THE EVENT.

I WAS HOPING YOU WOULD CO-MARSHAL.

PSH!

YOU'VE GOTTA BE KIDDING, TOM.

YOU'RE STILL TRYING TO TURN ME OVER TO THE DARK SIDE. TO SETTLE DOWN LIKE YOU.

WHEN YOU KNOW I'D STILL RATHER PLAY.

DAISY KUTTER
THE LAST TRAIN - Chapter One.

WRITTEN & ILLUSTRATED BY
KAZU KIBUISHI

IS THAT HER?

THAT'S WHAT THE BARTENDER SAYS.

SHE DOESN'T LOOK EVEN **HALF** AS MENACING AS I THOUGHT SHE WOULD. IN FACT, SHE LOOKS LIKE A TIRED OLD STICK.

WE STILL HAVE TO APPROACH WITH **EXTREME CAUTION.**

EXCUSE ME. YOU WOULDN'T HAPPEN TO BE THE INFAMOUS MISS DAISY KUTTER WOULD YOU?

YOUR REPUTATION IS **NOTORIOUS** IN THESE PARTS.

NOTORIOUS?

THEY SAY YOU SINGLE-HANDEDLY SHOT DOWN 15 SUPPLY FRIGATES OVER THE ADRIATIC SEA IN JUST A FEW MINUTES, BACK IN YORK'S WAR.

NOW, CONSIDERING YOU WERE ARMED WITH ONLY A SHOTGUN, I'D SAY THAT'S **IMPRESSIVE.**

IT WAS A **BIG** SHOTGUN. AND IT WAS ACTUALLY 16 FRIGATES IN 2 MINUTES AND 20 SECONDS. BUT WHO'S COUNTING?

CUT TO THE CHASE, BUDDY, WHAT DO YOU **WANT?**

I'M HERE TO OFFER YOU A JOB.

OUR EMPLOYER FINDS IT HARD TO BELIEVE YOU **CAN** QUIT.

PSH. WATCH ME.

GO TELL YOUR BOSS I'M NOT INTERESTED.

AND WHY THE HELL DOES HE WANT SOMEONE ROBBING HIS OWN TRAIN, ANYWAY?

SMELLS FISHY IF YOU ASK ME.

WE DON'T ASK QUESTIONS, LADY.

WELL, YOU SHOULD.

TRUST ME.

YOU SHOULD.

WELL, THE OFFER STILL STANDS.

WE'LL BE HERE IN TOWN FOR A WHILE. IF YOU CHANGE YOUR MIND, IT SHOULDN'T BE DIFFICULT TO FIND US.

SURE.

SHE'S TROUBLE. I CAN FEEL IT.

KEEP IT DOWN, WILL YA?

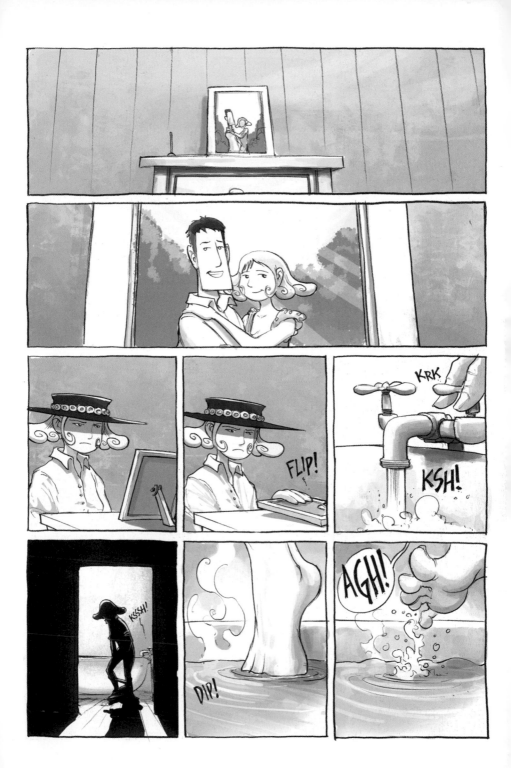

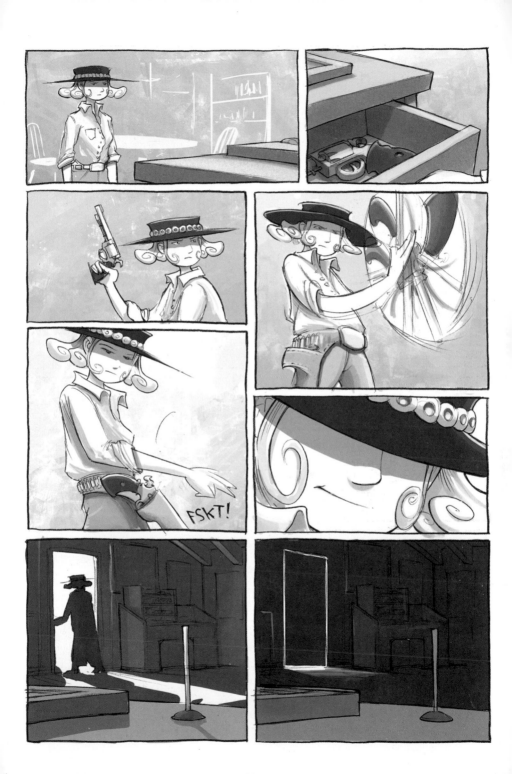

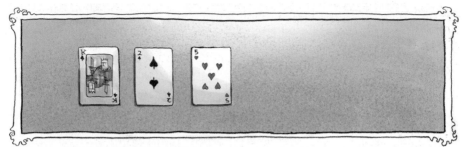

THE GAME IS **TEXAS HOLD 'EM**. EVERY PLAYER IS DEALT TWO CARDS FACE DOWN.
AFTER SEEING ONLY THESE CARDS, THE PLAYERS BEGIN THEIR FIRST ROUND OF
BETTING. AFTER EVERYONE BETS, THE DEALER PUTS THREE CARDS ON THE TABLE
FACE UP. THIS IS CALLED THE **"FLOP"**. THE PLAYERS SHARE THESE CARDS AND
THEY COMBINE THE TWO CARDS IN THEIR HAND WITH ANY THREE ON THE TABLE TO
MAKE THE BEST POSSIBLE FIVE-CARD POKER HAND.

THE FOURTH CARD, OR **"FOURTH STREET"**, AS IT'S CALLED, OFTEN CHANGES THE
DYNAMIC OF ANY GIVEN GAME. WHEN HAVING A KING MEANT YOU PROBABLY HAD
THE BEST HAND ON THE FLOP, FOURTH STREET SAID HAVING A TWO WAS EVEN
BETTER. WITH A TWO, YOU WOULD HAVE THREE OF A KIND, WHICH EASILY BEATS A
PAIR OF KINGS.

THE FIFTH CARD, OR **"THE RIVER"**, IS THE FINAL WORD. GAMES ARE QUITE OFTEN
WON OR LOST ON THE RIVER, SO BEFORE THAT FIFTH CARD APPEARS, IT IS
ALMOST ALWAYS ANYONE'S GAME. FOURTH STREET CROWNED THE TWO, BUT THE
RIVER SAID THE FIVE REIGNED SUPREME. IF YOU STUCK IT OUT WITH A FIVE IN
HAND, YOU'D BE SITTIN' REAL PRETTY RIGHT NOW. WITH THREE FIVES AND A PAIR
OF TWOS, YOU'D HAVE A FULL HOUSE NO ONE EXPECTED TO SEE BEFORE THE
RIVER CARD SHOWED UP. IN MOST GAMES, THIS WOULD BE ENOUGH TO ENSURE
VICTORY . . .

WHILE **LUCK** HAS PLENTY TO DO WITH YOUR CHANCES OF WINNING, THIS IS A GAME OF SKILL...

THE BEST PLAYERS BECOME **PSYCHOLOGISTS** AT THE CARD TABLE. READ YOUR OPPONENTS WELL, AND EXPONENTIALLY INCREASE YOUR CHANCES OF WINNING...

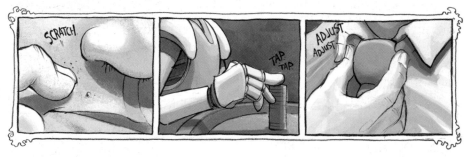

IT'S IMPORTANT TO WATCH FOR "**TELLS**". PLAYERS OFTEN GIVE SMALL SIGNS THROUGH PARTICULAR MANNERISMS THAT TELL YOU WHETHER THEY HAVE THE CARDS TO WIN, OR NOT. THESE ARE THE **TELLS**. BY WATCHING FOR THE TELLS, YOU CAN GAUGE YOUR CHANCES OF CALLING THEIR BLUFF. MANY OF THE BEST PLAYERS HIDE THEIR TELLS, MANY HAVE NONE, AND YET OTHERS EVEN USE THEM TO BLUFF THE COMPETITION.

THE BEST PLAYERS ALSO PLAY VERY **CONFIDENTLY**..

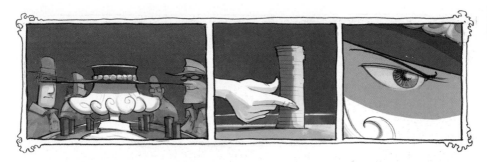

CONFIDENCE PLAYS A BIG PART IN THIS GAME. WITH IT, YOU CAN BLUFF EFFECTIVELY. BY SUPPRESSING IT, YOU CAN STRING PLAYERS IN FOR THE KILL AND HANG 'EM OUT TO DRY IF YOU HAVE THE CARDS TO WIN.

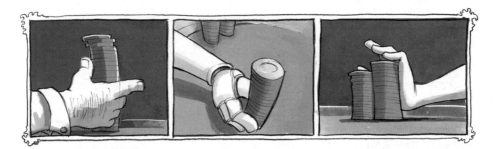

CONFIDENCE. IT'S YOUR MOST POWERFUL WEAPON. GOOD THING I HAVE IT IN SPADES . . .

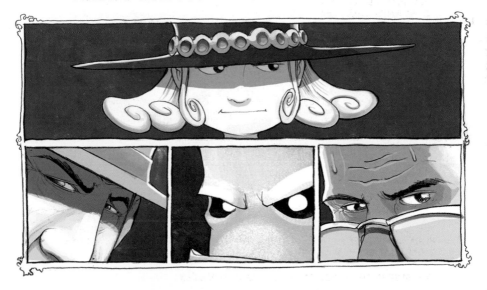

... AND FOR GOOD REASON.

FULL HOUSE. KINGS OVER FIVES. MISS KUTTER TAKES THE POT.

SORRY, BOYS.

DAMN FINE PLAY, MISS DAISY.

YES, VERY NICELY DONE.

LOOKS LIKE YOU HAVEN'T LOST YOUR TOUCH.

WHO ASKED YOU?

AND WHAT'S WITH THE RIDICULOUS BOY SCOUT GET-UP?

YOU MEAN THIS SCARF?

HEH. IT WAS A GIFT FROM DEPUTY MOSS. I THOUGHT IT WAS PRETTY COOL MYSELF.

SEEING AS HOW THE NIGHT'S OVER, YOU CAN RUN HOME AND RETIRE THAT THING BEFORE YOU SOIL YOUR REPUTATION.

THAT'S WHAT I CAME HERE TO TALK TO YOU ABOUT. THE NIGHT'S NOT OVER.

THERE'S STILL ONE MORE PLAYER.

DEALER

WHO IS HE?

SOME RICH OIL MAGNATE, I THINK.

IS HE GOOD?

HE'S BEEN PLAYING CALM AND COOL THE ENTIRE TIME.

HE PLAYED REAL CONSERVATIVE THE FIRST THREE QUARTERS OF THE LAST GAME. HE FOLDED ON ALMOST EVERY HAND. ONCE THERE WERE ONLY A COUPLE OTHERS LEFT AT THE TABLE, HE DESTROYED ANYONE WHO CHALLENGED HIM.

SSSIP.

HE EVEN HAD THE **SHORT** STACK.

SO HE'S A GOOD PLAYER. IF THE NIGHT WASN'T OVER, I WOULD HAVE SHOWN HIM A **BETTER** ONE.

CLAK! CLAK! CLAK!

BUT DAISY, HE'S ASKING THAT YOU PLAY A COUPLE OF HANDS.

TOO BAD.

TECHNICALLY SPEAKING, THIS IS A LAST MAN STANDING EVENT. YOU PLAY UNTIL THERE'S NO ONE ELSE LEFT. AND THAT RULE APPLIES UNLESS EVERYONE AGREES TO WALK AWAY. HE DOESN'T AGREE. HE WANTS TO PLAY.

SSSSIP.

WHOSE SIDE ARE YOU ON?!!

SMAK!

SORRY DAISY. RULES ARE RULES.

FINE. LET'S FINISH IT.

25

26

MISS KUTTER RAISES A THOUSAND BEFORE THE FLOP.

MISTER WINTERS SEES THE BET.

FNAP!

FNAP!

FNAP!

DEJA VU...

DEALER

MISS KUTTER RAISES ANOTHER 5,000 LUGS.

MR. WINTERS CALLS YOU, DAISY.

LET'S SEE WHAT YOU'VE GOT.

THREE KINGS.

THAT'S A VERY NICE HAND, MISS KUTTER.

UNFORTUNATELY, IT WON'T BE NICE ENOUGH TO WIN.

FLUSH BEATS A THREE-OF-A-KIND.

MR. WINTERS TAKES THE POT.

HEY DAISY, MAYBE YOU OUGHTTA—

SHUT UP, TOM.

DEALER, I'M GOING IN FOR 10,000.

?

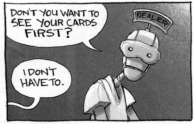

DON'T YOU WANT TO SEE YOUR CARDS FIRST?

DEALER

I DON'T HAVE TO.

OKAY THEN, MISS DAISY KUTTER IS IN 10,000 LUGS BEFORE THE FLOP.

WHAT'S SHE DOING, TOM?

TOSS!

TOSS!

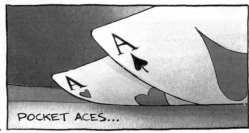

POCKET ACES...

IT'S HARD TO BE ANY MORE CONFIDENT AND NOT SHOW IT...

MAN, I'D LOVE TO WIPE THAT SMUG LOOK OFF HIS FACE WITH A BASEBALL BAT.

FOR NOW, A PAIR OF ACES IN THE HOLE WILL DO JUST FINE...

10,000 TO YOU, MR. WINTERS. JUST TO SEE THE FLOP.

DEALER

C'MON IN, YOU SMUG BASTARD.

FNAP!

DAMN IT.

MR. WINTERS, THE BET'S TO YOU.

I CHECK.

MISS KUTTER RAISES 5,000.

I'LL CALL AND I'LL **RAISE**.

BUT MISS KUTTER IS ALL IN, SHE—

NO.

I WANT TO GIVE MISS KUTTER A CHANCE TO **END IT RIGHT NOW.**

IF SHE STAKES HER STORE FOR THE REST OF THE BET, YOU CAN CONSIDER ME **ALL IN.** THAT'S 350,000 LUGS.

CAN HE DO THAT?

IT'S UP TO HER.

MISS KUTTER, IT'S YOUR CALL. YOU CAN ACCEPT THE BET OR PLAY FOR THE POT AS IS.

DAISY, DON'T—

FINE.

THE STORE FOR THE WIN.

I GUESS I'M REALLY ALL IN, NOW...

I HOPE YOU PLANNED TO TRAVEL LIGHT, MR. WINTERS.

FULL HOUSE. ACES OVER EIGHTS.

DID YOU THINK YOU WERE THE ONLY ONE WITH A POCKET PAIR?

FOUR-OF-A-KIND.

MR. WINTERS TAKES THE POT.

MY SINCEREST APOLOGIES, MISS KUTTER...

CHAPTER TWO

HEY, SHELLY'S CLOSING UP FOR THE NIGHT.

HE WANTS US OUT, NOW.

YOU SHOULDN'T HAVE BET THE STORE.

YOU THINK I DON'T ALREADY KNOW THAT?!

WELL, AT LEAST I KNOW YOU'RE ALL RIGHT IN THERE...

SHOVE IT, TOM!

THIS IS GETTING RIDICULOUS.

LEAVE ME ALONE.

I'M STAYING RIGHT HERE UNTIL I WAKE UP FROM THIS NIGHTMARE.

HEY TOM.
ARE YOU TAKING ME HOME OR NOT?

OH, SORRY MARCIE.

DEPUTY MOSS CAN ESCORT YOU HOME.

DEPUTY MOSS ALREADY LEFT.

WELL, IT LOOKS LIKE I'M STUCK HERE TAKING CARE OF A FRIEND.

SHE HAD A BAD NIGHT, SO I WANT TO MAKE SURE SHE'S OKAY.

I HOPE YOU DON'T MIND, MARCIE.

YOU'VE BEEN STANDING HERE FOR MORE THAN AN HOUR.

YEAH, HEH.

WELL, SHE CAN BE PRETTY STUBBORN.

THAT'S DAISY, ISN'T IT?

SHE'LL BE FINE TOM. JUST HAVE SHELLY TAKE HER HOME, IF SHE EVEN NEEDS AN ESCORT.

YEAH. I GUESS YOU'RE RIGHT.

HEY DAISY, I THINK MAY—

BDUMP!

I'M FINE. LET'S GO NOW.

WELL, WHAT ARE YOU WAITING FOR? CHOP CHOP!

IT'S STARTING TO RAIN...

SO NOW THAT YOU'VE PRETTY MUCH GAMBLED EVERYTHING AWAY, HAVE YOU THOUGHT ABOUT TAKING A JOB AT THE STATION?

I STILL DON'T SEE WHY YOU'RE SO AGAINST IT. THINK ABOUT IT... TAKING THE JOB COULD GET YOU OUT OF THIS HOLE YOU DUG FOR YOURSELF AND PAY YOUR BILLS. ON TOP OF THAT, YOU'D BE GREAT AT IT.

TOM, I'M SUPPOSED TO FIGHT COPS, NOT BE ONE.

WHO SAID YOU HAD TO DO THAT?

I STILL DON'T KNOW WHAT YOU'RE FIGHTING AGAINST.

DON'T YOU SEE? "THE MAN" DOESN'T EXIST. IT'S JUST ME.

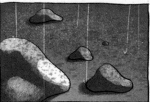

HWEEEEEE

LET ME SEE IF I CAN GET THAT RADIO STATION ON HERE.

ONE SUGAR, RIGHT?

OKAY, HERE WE GO.

GIRL FROM IPANEM

YOU SEE? IT'S BRAZILIAN JAZZ ALMOST ALL THE TIME.

JUST YESTERDAY, THEY WERE PLAYING YOUR FAVORITE SONG.

DESAFINADO.

"OUT OF TUNE"

THAT'S A GREAT PIECE.

HEY, I'VE BEEN MEANING TO ASK...

WHAT'S UP WITH THAT THING BEHIND YOU?

YOU MEAN THE BEAR? THAT WAS A GIFT FROM BURT.

SSSIP!..

HA HA! HE GAVE YOU A GIANT STUFFED BEAR?! THAT'S HILARIOUS!

HEY, IT WAS VERY SWEET OF HIM.

BEING AROUND SOME PEOPLE, I WASN'T REALLY ACCUSTOMED TO RECEIVING GIFTS.

...

SSSSSIP...

KNOCK KNOCK KNOCK

OH, WHAT THE HELL IS HE DOING HERE AGAIN? THIS IS THE FIFTH NIGHT IN A ROW.

WELL, I HEARD OLD BURT'S BEEN ON THE PROWL THESE LAST FEW WEEKS. SOMETHING ABOUT HIS EX-WIFE SHACKING UP WITH ONE OF THE FARMERS.

I JUST DIDN'T KNOW YOU WERE WHO HE WAS SO HOT FOR.

LISTEN BUDDY, IF YOU DON'T BEHAVE YOURSELF, I'M KICKING YOUR ASS OUT OF HERE. SO ACT COOL OKAY?

SURE SURE.

HELLO BURT.

HIYA, DAISY. I HAPPENED TO BE IN THE AREA. MAY I COME IN?

THIS MIGHT NOT BE THE BEST TIME. CAN I CALL YOU LATER?

OH, OKAY. CAN I AT LEAST MAKE A PHONE CALL?

I JUST NEED TO USE THE PHONE.

FINE. PLEASE MAKE IT QUICK.

THANK YOU KINDLY, MISS DAISY.

OH, HEY TOM.

HEY THERE BURT.

I'M GOING TO USE THE PHONE.

GO RIGHT AHEAD, BUDDY.

WHAT?!

FIRST OFF, NO FEET ON THE COUCH.

SECOND, YOU ACT LIKE A PRICK AND I BUST THAT RIDICULOUS CHIN OF YOURS.

GOT IT?

OKAY OKAY.

IS SOMETHING THE MATTER, BURT?

OH NO NO! NO, I JUST—

JUST GOTTA MAKE A PHONE CALL, UH... IT'S MY HORSE. SHE'S NOT FEELING WELL.

OH REALLY? I CAN TAKE A LOOK AT HER FOR YOU...

NO! ER, I MEAN, JUST THE PHONE CALL WILL DO!

IF YOU NEED ANYTHING ELSE JUST LET ME KNOW, OKAY?

THANKS, DAISY.

BOOP BOOP BEEP BEEP

UM, HI DOC.

THE NUMBER YOU HAVE DIALED IS NO LONGER IN USE OR IS DISCONNECTED. PLEASE HAN—

?

—UP OR DIAL AGAIN...

UM, YEAH, WELL, SHE'S DOING FINE.

HEY, I HAVE AN IDEA.

LET'S PLAY SOME FIVE CARD DRAW.

ARE YOU SERIOUS?

I'M TOTALLY SERIOUS.

PLAYING CARDS

WELL, I SUPPOSE I DON'T HAVE MUCH ELSE TO LOSE... WHAT ARE THE STAKES?

HOW ABOUT QUESTIONS?

PSH!

WINNER OF EACH HAND GETS TO ASK A QUESTION AND THE OTHER PLAYER HAS TO ANSWER HONESTLY.

WHAT ARE YOU UP TO, TOM?

C'MON. IT'LL BE FUN.

FINE. DEAL THOSE CARDS.

FpFpFpFpFpFpF

GET READY TO ANSWER SOME QUESTIONS, PAL.

OH, I'M READY.

PAIR OF KINGS.

TWO PAIR. ACES AND TENS.

I GO FIRST.

ARE YOU SEEING ANYONE BESIDES BURT?

NO.

HOW ABOUT THAT ONE SKINNY GUY?

THAT'S ANOTHER QUESTION. SHUFFLE THE DECK, PAL.

FSHTFSHTFS

ONE CARD PLEASE.

I'LL RAISE YOU ONE QUESTION.

FINE, I'LL SEE IT. WHAT HAVE YOU GOT?

NOTHING. I WAS BLUFFING.

THREE FIVES.

OKAY, I'M GOING STRAIGHT FOR THE JUGULAR.

SHOOT.

WHY DID YOU TAKE THAT STUPID JOB EVEN WHEN I ASKED YOU SPECIFICALLY NOT TO?

YOU MEAN BECOMING SHERIFF?

YEAH.

I DON'T THINK I CAN GIVE YOU A DEFINITE ANSWER, BUT I DO REMEMBER GOING THROUGH OUR SCRAPBOOK, READING ALL THE NEWS CLIPPINGS ABOUT OUR BONNIE AND CLYDE ROUTINE. I REMEMBER THINKING I'M GETTING TOO OLD TO KEEP GOING, AND I STARTED ENTERTAINING THE IDEA OF SWITCHING THINGS UP.

IT'S POSSIBLE I ALSO THOUGHT IT MIGHT EVEN BE A THRILLING CHALLENGE TO SEE WHAT IT FELT LIKE TO BE ON THE OTHER SIDE OF THE LAW. I GUESS I WAS CURIOUS.

AND?

IS THAT YOUR SECOND QUESTION?

NO.

I'LL ANSWER IT ANYWAY.

IT FEELS EXACTLY THE SAME.

I FEEL JUST AS GOOD.

AND JUST AS BAD.

OKAY, SECOND QUESTION.

WHY DO YOU STILL PUT UP WITH ME? I'M A NUISANCE, I ENDANGER YOUR JOB STATUS, AND EVER SINCE THE SPLIT I'VE TREATED YOU LIKE DIRT.

WHAT GIVES?

I THINK I STILL LOVE YOU.

PSH!!

YOU "THINK"?

YOU DON'T SOUND VERY SURE.

CRAP.

I'LL GO BREW MORE TEA.

IN THE MEANTIME, YOU SHUFFLE THAT DECK.

I CAME UP WITH MOR~

BAM!

AGH!!

STUPID SHELF!!

OH WOW, ARE YOU OKAY?

OOOOOHHH.

I'LL BE FINE. GO SHUFFLE SOME CARDS.

YOU'RE BLEEDING.

GET YOUR MIND OFF IT.

START WORRYING ABOUT YOUR REAL PROBLEMS, NOT YOUR OLD ONES.

SETTLE DOWN, DAISY. IT WASN'T HIS FAULT.

YOU'RE THE ONE THAT NEEDS COOLING DOWN...

YOU NEED A PLAN.

OKAY.

YOU NEED TO FIND THAT RAT BASTARD WHO TOOK YOUR STORE AND SHOOT HIM IN THE FACE.

SIGH

MAYBE TOM'S RIGHT...

59

CAREFUL WHAT YOU WISH FOR...

CAN WE OFFER YOU AN UMBRELLA?

NO THANKS.

I ASSUME YOU HAD SOME TIME TO RETHINK OUR BUSINESS PROPOSITION?

WHAT DO YOU MEAN? I HAVEN'T EVEN HAD A DAY.

MAN, YOU KIDS ARE DEMANDING.

YOUR BOSS IS ALSO ONE HELL OF A POKER PLAYER, BY THE WAY. IT TOOK ME A WHILE TO PUT TWO AND TWO TOGETHER. YOU GUYS ARE GRIFTERS.

HEH.

I WOULDN'T SAY THAT, MISS KUTTER. A MATTER OF BAD LUCK AND COINCIDENCE IS ALL.

MR. WINTERS WOULD LIKE TO APOLOGIZE FOR THE UNUSUAL CIRCUMSTANCES.

HAD HE KNOWN YOU WERE WORKING WITH US HE WOULD HAVE FOLDED AND WALKED AWAY.

BULLSHIT.

HE HAD ME MARKED FROM THE BEGINNING.

AND WHO SAID I WAS WORKING WITH YOU?

OH, THAT'S RIGHT. SHE DOESN'T WORK WITH MACHINES, REMEMBER?

SHUT UP, BLOOM. YOU'RE NOT HELPING.

MACHINES, GRIFTERS, AND <u>CLOWNS</u>. I DON'T WORK WITH ANY OF THEM.

I GET THE IMPRESSION YOU BOYS QUALIFY FOR ALL THREE.

THIS IS A LEGITIMATE JOB, MISS KUTTER, AND WE NEED YOUR HELP. YOU'RE RIGHT IN ASSUMING WE'RE A BIT WET BEHIND THE EARS, BUT THIS IS WHY YOU'RE A NECESSARY COMPONENT FOR THE JOB. YOU'RE THE EXPERT. YOU HAVE THE TALENT, AND YOU'RE THE ONLY ONE WHO CAN HELP US DO THIS RIGHT...

MR. WINTERS ALSO AGREED TO RETURN THE STORE AND POKER WINNINGS <u>ON TOP</u> OF THE INITIAL 350,000 LUGS HE OFFERED IF YOU TAKE THE JOB.

LET ME GET THIS STRAIGHT. HE WANTS TO PAY ME TO ROB HIS OWN STUPID TRAIN?

IF YOU GUYS <u>AREN'T</u> GRIFTERS, THEN WHAT'S THE CATCH?

MR. WINTERS DEALS IN SECURITY SYSTEMS. HE IS THE WORLD'S LEADING MANUFACTURER OF LOCKS, AND VAULTS. HE ALSO PRODUCES ALARMS AND SECURITY ROBOTS.

RECENTLY, THE WINTERS LOCK COMPANY UNVEILED ITS NEW, STATE-OF-THE-ART RAILROAD SECURITY GUARD. IT IS, AS MY CLIENT INSISTS, FOOLPROOF.

HOWEVER, DURING A MEETING OF THE COMPANY'S CHIEF OFFICERS, A PARTNER CLAIMED THAT NO SECURITY DEVICES ARE TRULY FOOLPROOF. HE MENTIONED YOU AS AN EXAMPLE OF HOW THIS MAY BE THE CASE.

NEEDLESS TO SAY, MR. WINTERS GREW VERY UPSET.

IN RESPONSE TO THIS STATEMENT, MR. WINTERS PROPOSED TO HIRE DAISY KUTTER HERSELF TO TEST THE INTEGRITY OF THE GUARD. HE CLAIMS YOU CAN'T GET PAST IT. WE THINK OTHERWISE.

AND NOW, HERE WE ARE.

IT WOULD BE AN HONOR TO WORK BESIDE YOU, MISS KUTTER, AND IT WOULD BE THE FULFILLMENT OF ONE OF MY CAREER GOALS.

OF COURSE, WITHOUT YOUR INVOLVEMENT, THIS JOB DOESN'T EXIST.

IF YOU CHOOSE NOT TO ACCEPT THE JOB, WE WILL BE SENT HOME, NONE THE RICHER.

SO NOW THE TRUTH COMES OUT.

YOU SAPS NEED ME TO EVEN GET THE JOB.

I WAS WONDERING WHAT YOUR ANGLE WAS...

LISTEN, LADY. WE SPENT A SMALL FORTUNE JUST TO FIND YOU. IF WE'RE SENT BACK OUT ON THE STREET WITHOUT COMPENSATION, SOMEONE'S GONNA PAY ONE WAY OR ANOTHER.

CATCH MY DRIFT?

GOOD TO HAVE YOU ABOARD, MISS KUTTER.

WE'LL BRIEF YOU ON THE JOB TOMORROW AT NOON.

PLEASE MEET US AT CROW'S PEAK AND WE CAN GO FROM THERE.

IF YOU HAVE ANY QUESTIONS OR CONCERNS, PLEASE ADDRESS THEM.

I USUALLY WORK ALONE.

IF I HAVE ANY CONCERNS RIGHT NOW, IT'S SIMPLY YOU TWO. I GET THE FEELING YOU'RE IN OVER YOUR HEAD.

DON'T WORRY ABOUT US, MISS KUTTER, WE KNOW WHAT WE'RE DOING.

I GET THE FEELING THIS WILL ALL TURN OUT RIGHT IN THE END.

SEE YOU AT NOON.

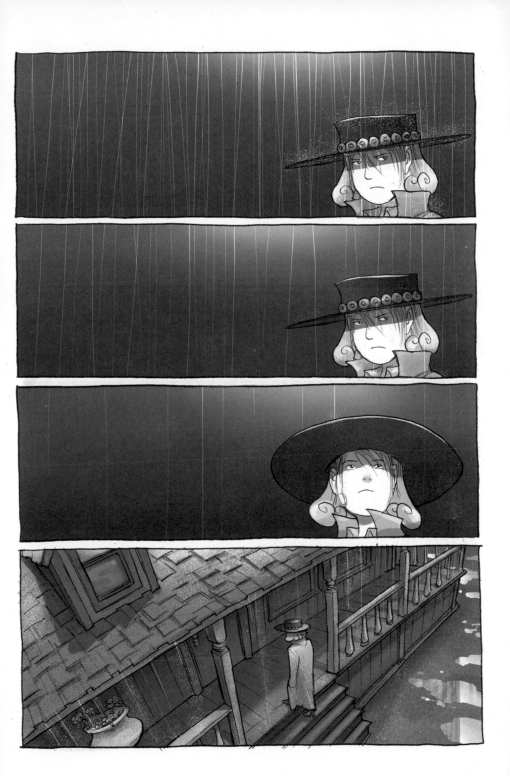

NEVER ROBBED A TRAIN WITH NO MONEY IN IT BEFORE.

HEH. NEVER THOUGHT OF IT THAT WAY.

TECHNICALLY, THAT'S TRUE.

BUT YOU'D BE REMISS NOT MENTIONING THE GOBS OF CASH WE'LL BE WALKING AWAY WITH IN THE END.

SHE LOOKS LIKE SHE'S HAVING SECOND THOUGHTS.

BLOOM, THERE ARE PLENTY OF THINGS IN LIFE I'M REALLY UNSURE ABOUT...

CHAPTER THREE

WAIT A MINUTE. THAT'S IT?!

WHAT DID YOU EXPECT?

I JUST WASN'T EXPECTING IT TO BE SO... SIMPLE.

A SIMPLE PLAN IS BEST.

YOU CAN COUNT ON IT GETTING COMPLICATED IN THE END.

YES, BUT YOU... YOU'RE CONSIDERED BY MANY TO BE THE BEST STRATEGIST OUTSIDE THE MILITARY... GENERALS STUDY YOUR HEISTS LIKE THEY WERE TEXTBOOKS.

I'VE WAITED A LONG TIME TO SEE HOW YOU WORK, TO PICK YOUR BRAIN... AND YOU PRESENT US...

...WITH THIS! HAH!
SORRY TO DISAPPOINT YOU BUDDY...
PLAN...
Daisy (me) runs to end of train and runs back to front on roof
robot bad guys
SAFE
Morris and Bloom (you guys) disconnect other cars.
Disconnect
you guys.
money!

BUT THAT'S JUST THE WAY I WORK.

I'M NOT SURE IF I'M DISAPPOINTED OR IMPRESSED.

BUT IN ANY CASE, I AM DEFINITELY ENTERTAINED.

I NEED A DRINK.

PLAN.

I LIKE THIS PLAN.

IT'LL WORK.

OF COURSE IT'LL WORK.

YOU TOASTERS ARE EASY TO READ.

YOU'RE SIMPLE VERSIONS OF US.

SHUFFLE SHUFFLE

YOU ARE ONE FUNNY RATTLESNAKE, LADY.

YOU'VE GOT BITE, BUT I LIKE YA.

DON'T GROW TOO CLOSE, BUD.

YOU WOULDN'T WANT TO GET **BIT.**

I KNEW SHE HAD A PROBLEM WITH MACHINES. I COULD TELL RIGHT AWAY.

WILL YOU TWO CUT THAT OUT?

WE'VE GOT WORK TO DO.

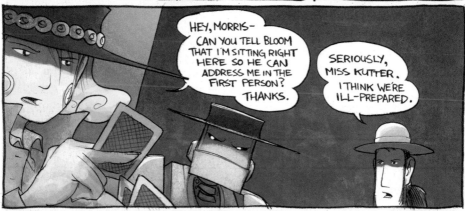

HEY, MORRIS— CAN YOU TELL BLOOM THAT I'M SITTING RIGHT HERE SO HE CAN ADDRESS ME IN THE FIRST PERSON? THANKS.

SERIOUSLY, MISS KUTTER. I THINK WE'RE ILL-PREPARED.

WELL, THAT'S A GIVEN CONSIDERING OUR SCHEDULE.

THE BEST THING TO DO NOW IS JUST **RELAX** AND HOPE FOR THE BEST.

BESIDES, AS LONG AS WE DON'T DEAL WITH ANYTHING COMPLETELY UNEXPECTED, WE'LL BE **FINE.**

THE NEXT DAY...

HI DAISY.

WHAT THE HELL ARE YOU DOING HERE, TOM?

I'M ON VACATION.

GIVE ME A BREAK.

I JUST THOUGHT I COULD USE A TRAIN RIDE OUT TO THE COUNTRY.

YOU KNOW, SEE STUFF.

HOW'D YOU FIND OUT?

FIND OUT? ABOUT WHAT?

STOP PLAYING AROUND.

YOU KNOW WHAT I'M TALKING ABOUT.

73

WELL THAT'S ALWAYS THE PROBLEM, ISN'T IT?

I NEVER KNOW WHAT YOU'RE TALKING ABOUT.

YOU'VE NEVER BEEN STRAIGHTFORWARD WITH ME.

THAT'S BECAUSE YOU NEVER UNDERSTAND!

UNDERSTAND WHAT?

SEE?!

FORGET IT TOM.

AND I SUGGEST STAYING OFF THIS TRAIN.

WHY?

YOU GOING TO ROB IT OR SOMETHING?

OOOOOOHH!

WHOA! HEY!

EASY THERE TIGER.

I SAID I WAS ON VACATION.

AND I MEAN IT.

LOOK, I'M NOT WEARING A BADGE.

I'M OFF DUTY.

JUST PROMISE ME ONE THING.

TELL ME IT'S THE LAST ONE.

LET GO.

DAISY...

I CAN'T LET YOU KEEP DOING THIS.

WHY NOT? JUST IGNORE ME. NOT LIKE YOU HAVEN'T DONE IT BEFORE.

I'M THE SHERIFF. I LET YOU DO THIS AND I'M NOT A VERY GOOD ONE.

DAMN IT, TOM!

WHO WAS THAT JERK?

WE CAN TAKE CARE OF HIM, IF YOU WANT.

LEAVE HIM BE.

HE'S HARMLESS.

SO WHAT ARE WE UP AGAINST?

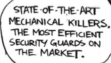

MR. WINTERS HAS ARMED THE TRAIN WITH HIS MOST LETHAL SECURITY ROBOTS.

STATE-OF-THE-ART MECHANICAL KILLERS. THE MOST EFFICIENT SECURITY GUARDS ON THE MARKET.

THEY'VE TAKEN DOWN SOME OF THE FIERCEST BANDITS IN THE LAND, AS I'M SURE YOU'VE HEARD.

SECURITY   SECURITY   SECURITY

YOU'VE GOTTA BE KIDDING.

HM. THEY DO LOOK LIKE THE OLD MODELS.

HOWEVER, DON'T BE FOOLED BY THE FRIENDLY FACADE.

UNDER THE SURFACE, THEY ARE RUTHLESS KILLING MACHINES.

LIKE LIONS.

CALM THOSE NERVES, MORRIS. I'VE BEEN DOING THIS FOR YEARS.

AND WE MAY AS WELL START COUNTING OUR CHICKENS.

CHICKENS?

WE'RE OVER THE BRIDGE. THAT'S OUR CUE, BOYS.

I JUST NEED FIVE MINUTES. I THINK I CAN EVEN RUN THE LENGTH OF THE TRAIN IN UNDER THREE.

YOU KNOW WE HAVE YOU COVERED.

JUST DON'T GET KILLED.

I WON'T. NOW IF YOU BOYS WILL EXCUSE ME...

SPANG!

..BACK UP...
..I NEED BACK UP...

PLEASE DON'T...

SORRY PAL.

HERE COMES THE CALVARY.

I'LL CATCH YA BOYS LATER.

CLICK!

BAM!

CRAK!

BAM BAM!

STOP RIGHT THERE!

BAM!

SPAK!

BAM!

SPAK!

HEY, NO RUNNING!

SORRY!

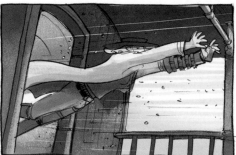
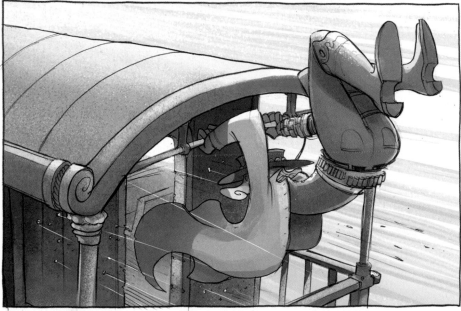

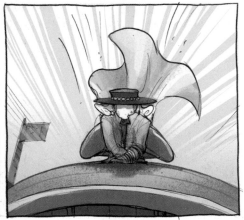

ADIOS AMIGOS.

THEY'RE NOT EVEN SHOOTING AT US.

AH, RELAX.

YOU OKAY?

HEH.

WOOHOOO!

CONGRATS, GENTLEMEN, ON MAKING THE EASIEST SMALL FORTUNE YOU'RE EVER BOUND TO MAKE.

THAT DOESN'T BOTHER YOU?

VERY IMPRESSIVE, DAISY. YOU HAVEN'T LOST YOUR TOUCH.

THANK YOU, MR. MCKAY.

BY THE WAY, I BROUGHT YOU SOMETHING. JUST IN CASE.

THAT'S THE SHOTGUN, ISN'T IT?

I HAD A FEELING YOU MIGHT NEED IT.

THANKS, BUT I THINK I'VE GOT IT HANDLED.

YOU MAKE A PRETTY LOUSY SHERIFF, MR. MCKAY.

THAT'S WHY I'M LOOKING FOR A GOOD DEPUTY.

HEY, WHERE YOU GOING?

I'M CHECKING THE SAFE.

I THOUGHT THERE WAS NOTHING IN THERE.

WOULDN'T HURT TO CHECK, RIGHT? WE'VE GOT SOME TIME TO KILL BEFORE WE GET TO NEEDLES.

MIGHT BE NICE IF WE FOUND OURSELVES A NICE BONUS, DON'T YOU THINK?

YOU'RE A GREEDY LITTLE RAT... WE'LL SPLIT IT 50-50.

HELLO?

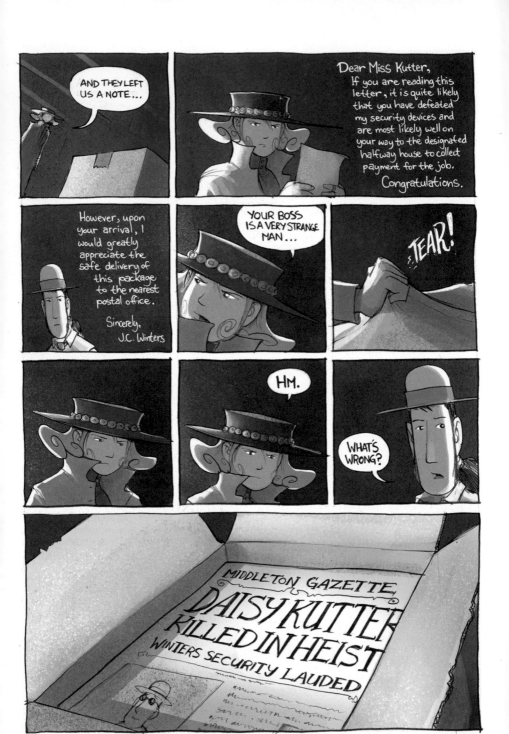

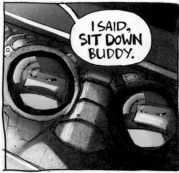

94

BLOOM,
NOOO!

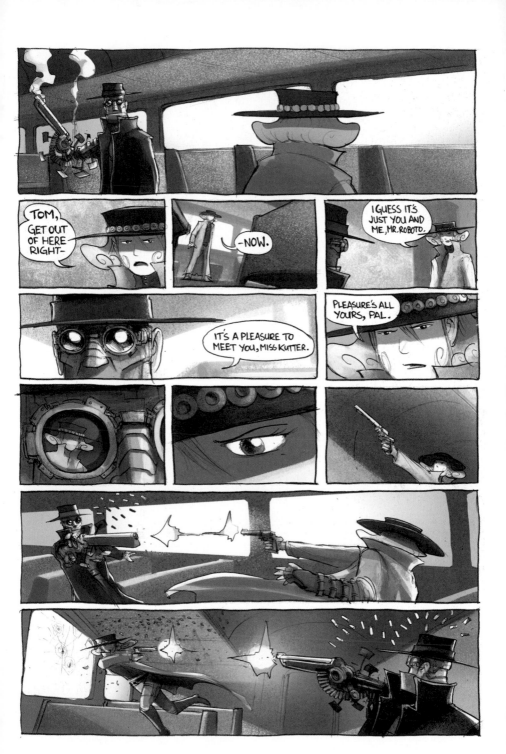

HEY BUDDY--

CLIK

KRAK

KOOOM!!

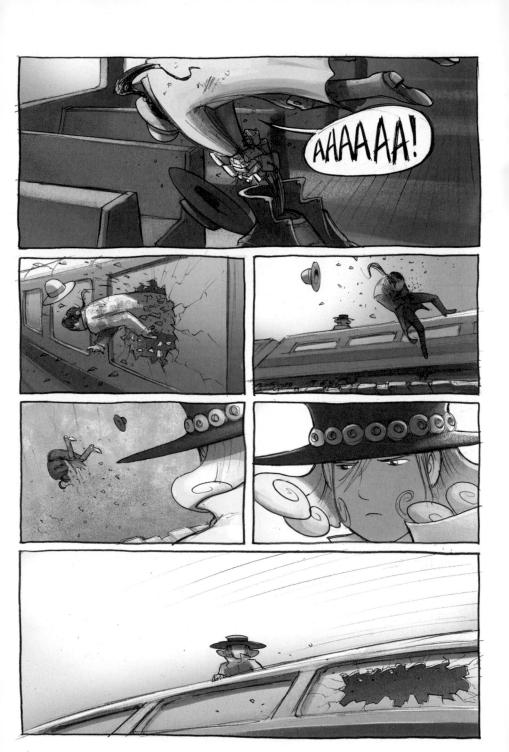

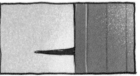

BAM!
BAM!

SPAK!

SPAK!

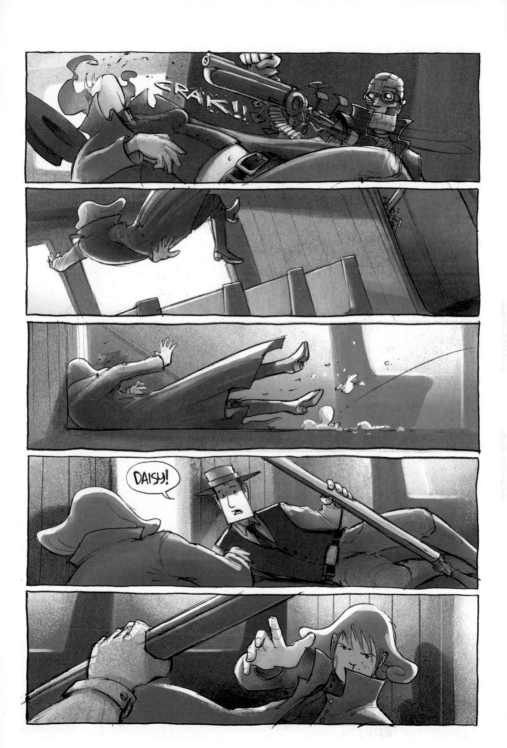

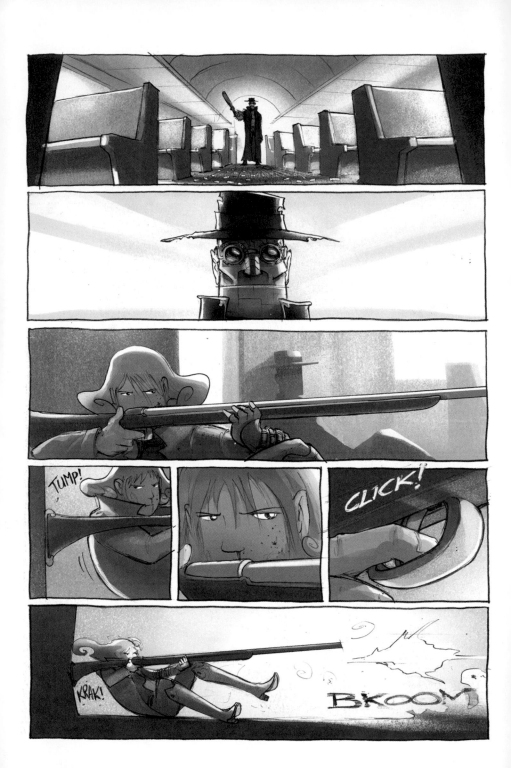

CHAPTER FOUR

IT'S BEEN A WHILE SINCE I'VE BEEN BACK HERE...

HEY— WHERE ARE YOU GOING, DAISY?

TO COLLECT MY CHECK.

AND GET MY STORE BACK.

YOU REALLY THINK THIS CLOWN IS GOING TO PAY YOU?

YES.

RIGHT AFTER I SHOOT THE BASTARD IN THE FACE.

YOU PLAN ON STOPPING ME?

I TOLD YOU...

I TAGGED ALONG TO MAKE SURE YOU WERE SAFE.

THAT'S IT.

I'M NOT GOING TO STOP YOU FROM DOING ANYTHING, BUT DON'T DO SOMETHING WE'LL BOTH REGRET.

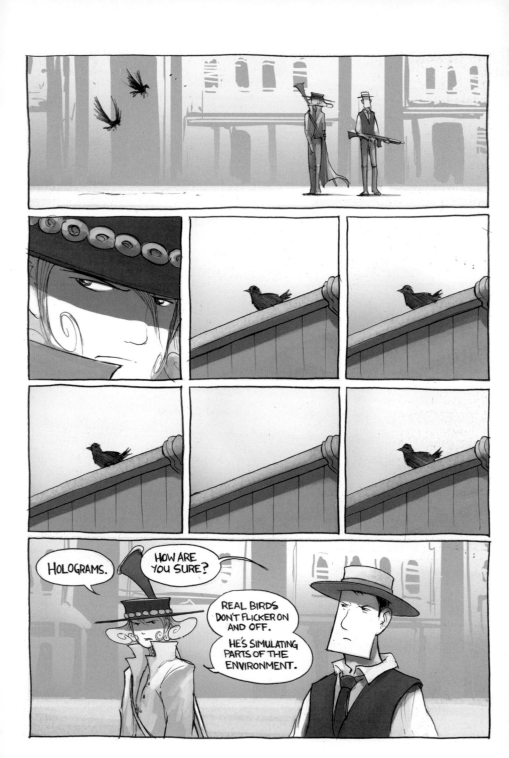

SEEKING TARGET

LOCK

UNGH!

THUP! THUP! THUP!

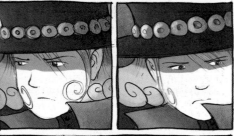

TOM!

WE HAVE TO GET OUT OF HERE. HE'LL MOW US DOWN.

DAISY, I CAN'T MOVE MY LEGS.

YOU'RE PROBABLY JUST IN SHOCK.

I SURE HOPE YOU'RE RIGHT.

RIIIPPP

HOLD STILL.

YOU HAVE TO GET UP, TOM. IF I HAVE TO CARRY YOU, WE CAN'T MOVE FAST ENOUGH.

JUST LEAVE ME HERE FOR NOW.

SHOOT THAT BASTARD IN THE FACE THEN GET BACK HERE BEFORE I BLEED TO DEATH.

TOM,

I ONLY HAVE ONE MORE SHELL.

THAT'S ALL YOU NEED.

I'VE SEEN THAT MECH BEFORE.

IT'S NOT A NEW MODEL AND IT'S DEFINITELY **NOT** CONTROLLED REMOTELY.

HE'S IN THERE.

HE'S PILOTING THAT THING.

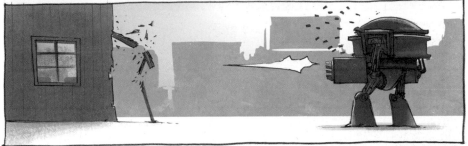

C'MON, TOM! WE HAVE TO MOVE!!

NO, DAISY, WAIT—

AAAGH!

I'LL BE RIGHT BACK.

OH, I DON'T DOUBT THAT.

I'M JUST WONDERING HOW LONG YOU'LL BE AWAY THIS TIME.

TEN MINUTES.

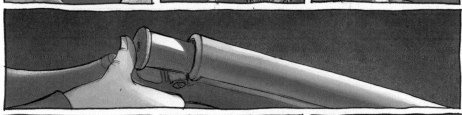

HEH. TEN?

THAT SOUNDS LIKE A MILLENNIUM ON DAISY TIME.

I'M GETTING OLD, TOM.

WE BOTH ARE.

GOOD LUCK, DAISY.

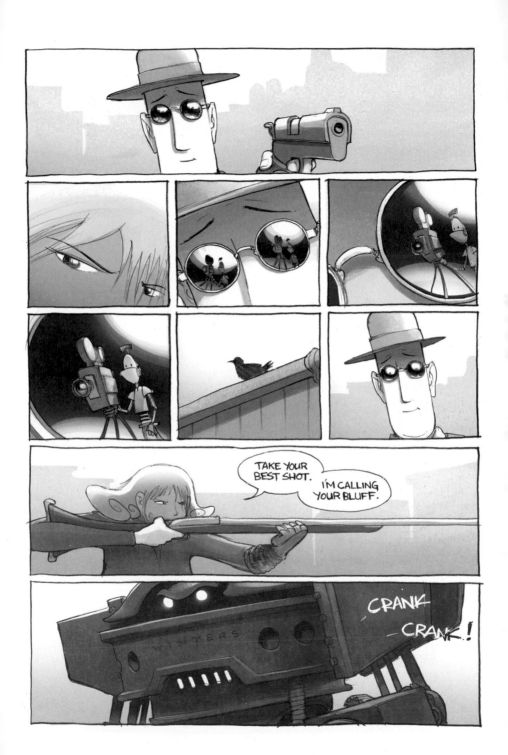

PLIP!

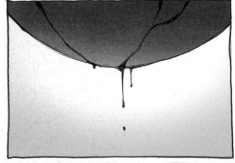

PLIP!

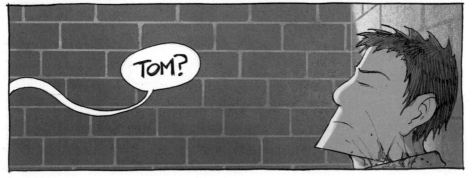

144

145

SO THAT WAS THE
SUMMER TOM LOST
THE ABILITY TO WALK.

HE NEVER REMINDED ME
THAT IT WAS MY FAULT.

IN FACT, I DON'T EVEN
THINK HE FEELS THAT WAY.

THAT'S JUST THE
KIND OF GUY HE IS...

SO WHAT DID THE DOCTOR SAY?

WELL, THE PROGNOSIS WASN'T GOOD,

BUT YOU KNOW I THINK THOSE GUYS ARE FULL OF IT.

THE DOC SAID IT'S LIKELY HE WON'T WALK AGAIN.

YEAH, BUT THAT QUACK ALSO SAID I WAS CLINICALLY DEPRESSED. ME.

CAN YOU BELIEVE THAT?

ANYWAY, I WON'T LET A DOCTOR TELL ME WHAT I CAN OR CAN'T DO. I'LL BE BACK UP SOON.

OF COURSE YOU WILL.

IN FACT, YOU'LL HAVE TO...

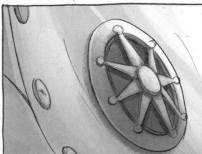

SINCE YOU CAN BE DAMN SURE THIS IS ONLY TEMPORARY.

POKER
NIGHT

AW, COME ON, DAISY.

HEY, YOU'RE SUPPOSED TO BE MARSHALLING THE EVENT, NOT PARTICIPATING.

OH, LIGHTEN UP. IT'S JUST A COUPLE OF HANDS.

I'M ALMOST FINISHED, ANYWAY. JUST LET ME CLEAN THESE GUYS OUT AND I'LL GET BACK ON DUTY...

SIGH

HEH. YOU'RE THE BEST.

SOMETIMES, EVEN WHEN YOU'RE DEALT A SURE HAND...

THINGS CAN TAKE AN UNEXPECTED TURN...

AND LEAVE YOU SECOND GUESSING...

THERE'S ALWAYS THE OPTION TO FOLD...

...OR STICK WITH IT.

I'LL CALL.

UNCERTAINTY CAN GET TO SOME PEOPLE...

DEALER

IT CAN AGITATE THEM...

FNAP!

10

IT CAN PARALYZE THEM.

FNAP!

10

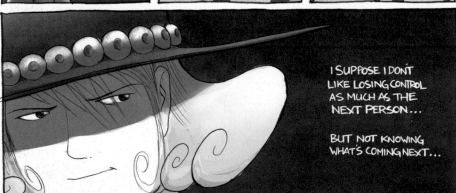

I SUPPOSE I DON'T LIKE LOSING CONTROL AS MUCH AS THE NEXT PERSON...

BUT NOT KNOWING WHAT'S COMING NEXT...

INTRODUCING DAISY KUTTER

It actually feels funny to be writing about this novel. Only a couple of years back, if someone told me I would be drawing a graphic novel about a skinny blonde gunfighter in a world full of robots, I would have laughed. Somewhere between then and now, I drew a little sketch of a cowgirl and posted it on The Drawing Board, an online illustration forum where a lot of very talented illustrators would meet and share their work. Since then, her world continued to develop and I found myself wanting to tell more of her story with each new illustration I shared with the other artists. The thought of tackling a project like The Last Train hadn't crossed my mind.

A couple of months after drawing the first image, I went on a trip to Las Vegas, and was surrounded by the chaos of cultures from around the world coming together in such a strange, and somewhat garish, way. Yet there were tons of people, my friends and family included, that loved this kind of atmosphere. I suppose that despite my initial aversion to this outlandish environment, this place (or at least this strange country) is what I would have to call home.

Thinking back on the character of Daisy, I realized that this is the attitude that she would take. She would be someone who could sit in the middle of a raging storm unmoved, accepting the craziness surrounding her. The most turbulent aspects of her life would actually play out in her private life, in her emotions, and it would be juxtaposed with the calm, cool way she handles an extraordinarily wild situation in her physical reality. Her emotions would also serve as the catalyst for many of the storms that get brewed up, and would lead us on a roller coaster ride fraught with danger and excitement. It was these elements that made Daisy Kutter the project I most wanted to do, however unlikely.

One of my big secrets is that I don't enjoy the act of drawing all that much, but making my way through this book has been tremendous fun. I just love finding out more about this complex and wonderful human being, and I'm looking forward to seeing what she does next. I hope you all enjoyed this book, and please have fun going through my sketches and the wonderful pin-up art by my friends!

EARLY **DAISY**

These are the first two drawings of Daisy
that were posted on The Drawing Board.
She's come quite a long way since then...

The Daisy pics on the previous two
pages were the third and fourth
drawings of the gunslinging young lady,
and where the elements of a story
started to appear. In fact, *The Last Train*
was essentially supposed to be the fifth
image of Daisy, with her on the outside
of a train, thwarting a heist. I basically
worked my way through the story to get
to draw that one image in my head.
However, when I got there, I drew something else.

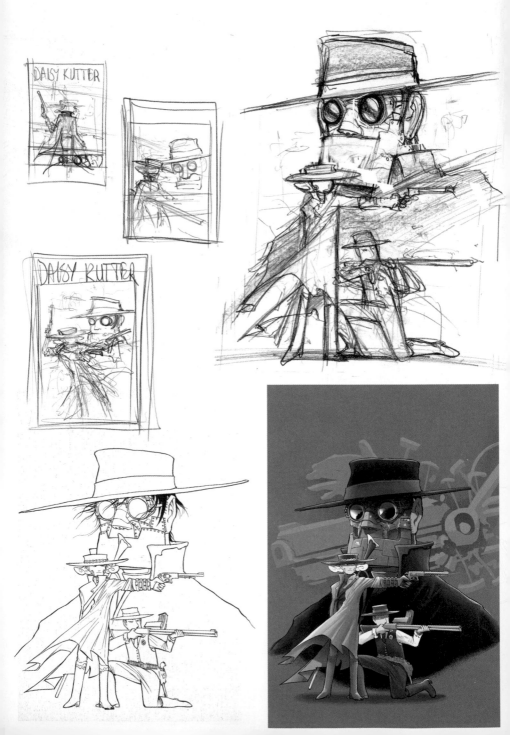

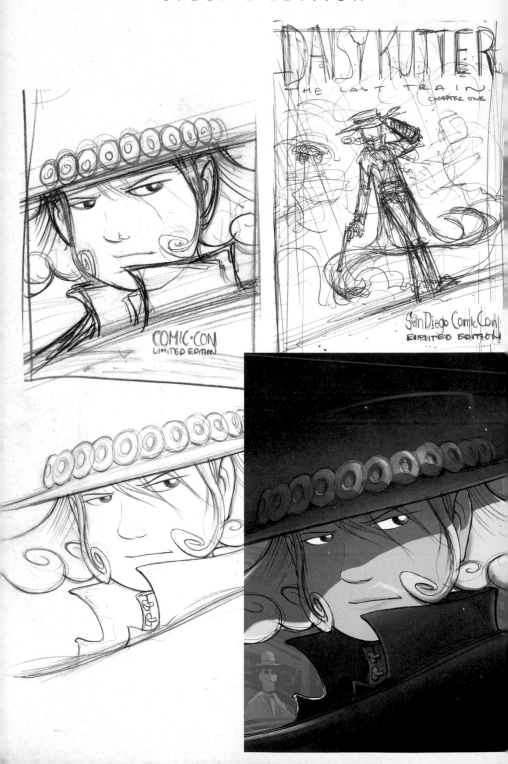

CHAPTER ONE

PROCESS

1. **The writing stage.** Since I let the pictures do a lot of the talking in Daisy Kutter, I like to write the pages as a series of thumbnails. These scribbly notes serve as both the script and visual guideline for the layouts. Each page is approximately 3 inches by 2 inches in size.

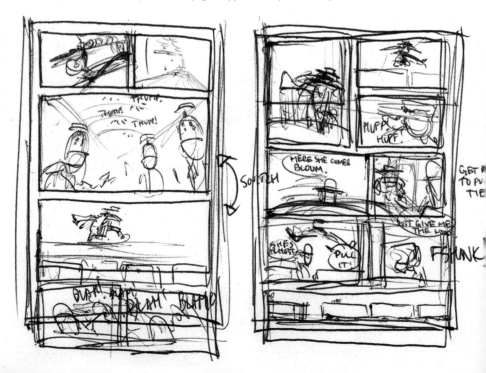

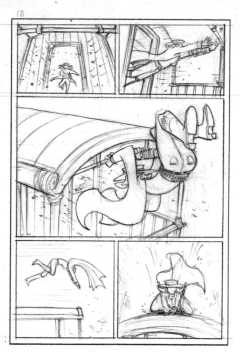

2. **The layout stage.** During the adaptation of the rough thumbnail pages, the composition and dialogue are adjusted and the pages get close to the final output. These pages are approximately 6.5 by 4.5 inches in size.

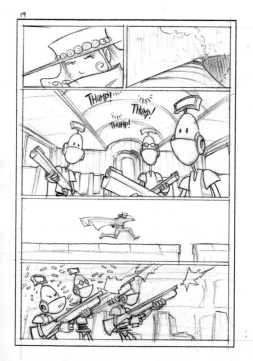

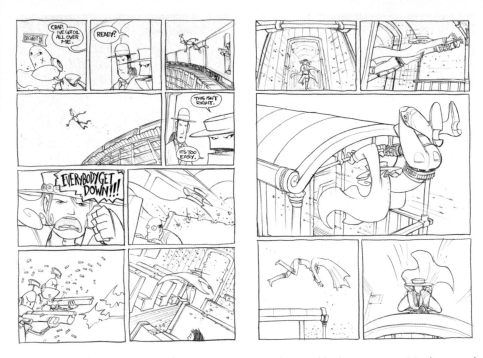

3. **The penciling stage.** The rough layouts are either printed out as a blue line image onto Bristol paper and drawn over with a pencil, or they are printed out in black ink and these pages are redrawn over them on a light table. This is the phase where all linework is cleaned up. The originals are drawn on 11x14 inch Bristol with a regular 2B pencil

4. **The blocking stage.** Before moving on to the painting stage, the characters, the objects, and the backgrounds are filled in with opaque colors in Photoshop, and are set on separate layers. This makes selecting specific areas much easier. My friends helped me out tremendously at this stage. These particular examples were blocked in by Tony Cliff and Richard Pose. Thanks guys!

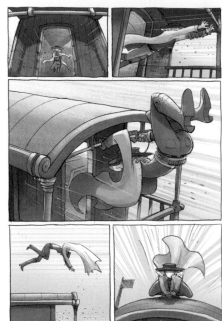

5. **The painting stage.** This is the final stage in the process, and it's where tones and textures are used to add depth and volume to the images. Much of the work in this phase goes into balancing the tones and lighting the scene to best fit the mood. Since much of this is based initially on guesswork and playing off of happy accidents, it can be the most enjoyable, yet at the same time the most tedious, part of the process.

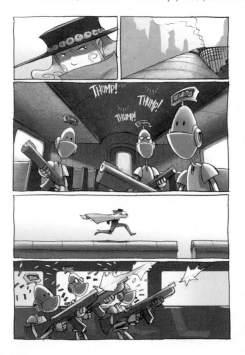

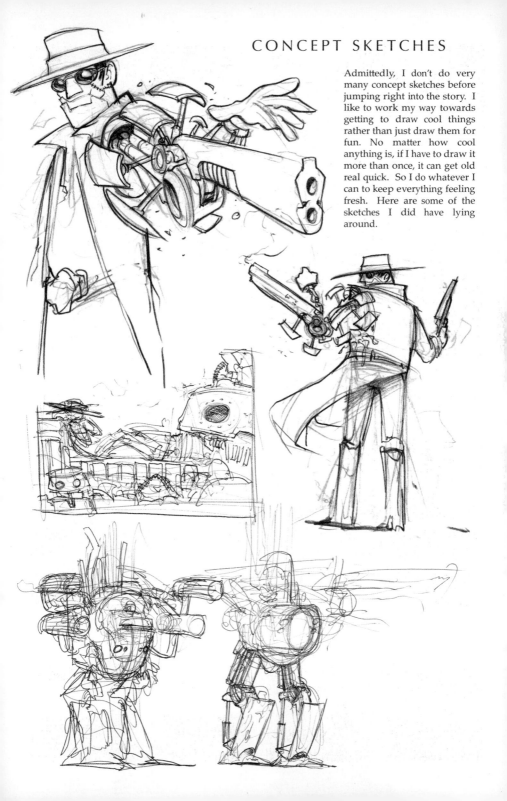

CONCEPT SKETCHES

Admittedly, I don't do very many concept sketches before jumping right into the story. I like to work my way towards getting to draw cool things rather than just draw them for fun. No matter how cool anything is, if I have to draw it more than once, it can get old real quick. So I do whatever I can to keep everything feeling fresh. Here are some of the sketches I did have lying around.

PIN-UP GALLERY

RAD **SECHRIST**

BILL PRESING

CHRIS **APPELHANS**

CATIA **CHIEN**

PHIL CRAVEN

NICOLAS **SEIGNERET**

"BANNISTER"

HOPE **LARSON**

KEAN **SOO**

김지훈 '04

DEREK **KIRK KIM**

CLIO **CHIANG**

JEN **WANG**

AMY KIM **GANTER**

BENJAMIN **PLOUFFE**

L FRANK **WEBER**

JAKE **PARKER**

RICHARD **POSE**

JOANA **CARNEIRO**

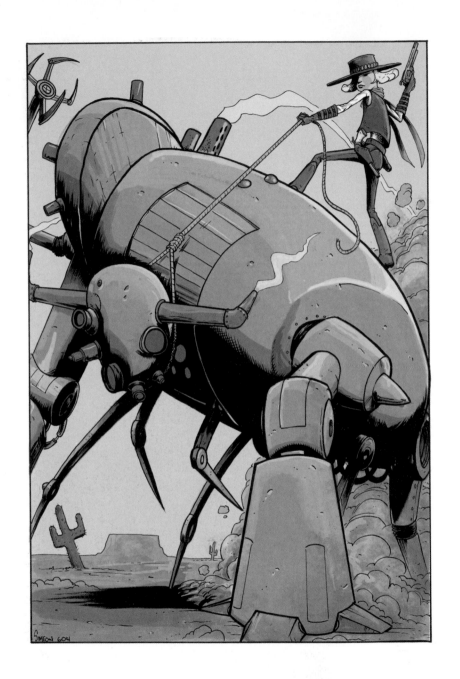

SIMEON **WILKINS**

D O U G L A S **H O L G A T E**

EUAN **MACTAVISH**

RODOLPHE **GUENODEN**

BEN **CALDWELL**

Extra Special Thanks to:

Phil Craven, Jake Parker, Rad Sechrist, Kean Soo, Tony Cliff, Nicolas Seigneret, Wira Winata, Andy Runton, Chris Appelhans, Clio Chiang, Richard Pose, Douglass Holgate, and Shadi Muklashy for assisting me in producing these books. You're all so awesome, and I would have been screwed if it weren't for you guys and gals.

Thanks also to:

Scott McCloud, Neil Babra, Khang Le, David Desmarais, Eric Wu, Rusty Yates, Catia Chien, John Bitterolf, Joe Palladino, everyone on the FLIGHT crew, Amy Yu, Amy Kim Ganter, Derek Kirk Kim, Ben Zhu at Nucleus, George and the rest of the crew at The Comics Factory, Taka, Julie, Emi, Mom, Dad, Bobby, Grandpa, and of course, Grandma!

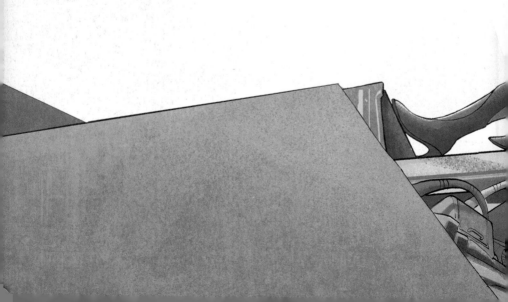

ALSO AVAILABLE FROM VIPER COMICS

WWW.VIPERCOMICS.COM

DEAD@17: THE COMPLETE FIRST SERIES (REPRINT)
ISBN: 0-9754193-0-7

DEAD@17: BLOOD OF SAINTS
ISBN: 0-9754193-1-5

DEAD@17: REVOLUTION
ISBN: 0-9754193-3-1

THE EXPENDABLE ONE
ISBN: 0-9754193-9-0

THE MIDDLEMAN: THE TRADE PAPERBACK IMPERATIVE
ISBN: 0-9754193-7-4

RANDOM ENCOUNTER: VOLUME 1
ISBN: 0-9754193-8-2

ODDLY NORMAL: VOLUME 1
ISBN: 0-9777883-0-X

YOU'LL HAVE THAT: VOLUME 1
ISBN: 0-9777883-1-8

EMILY EDISON
ISBN: 0-9777883-2-6

THE MIDDLEMAN: THE SECOND VOLUME INEVITABILITY
ISBN: 0-9777883-4-2